Something for School @ 2006 by Lee, Hyun Young
This translated edition is published by arrangement with Sakyejul Publishing Ltd.
English Edition © 2008 by Kane/Miller Book Publishers, Inc.

Library of Congress Control Number: 2008920671
Printed and bound in China
1 2 3 4 5 6 7 8 9 10

ISBN: 978-1-933605-85-2

Something for School

Kane/Miller
BOOK PUBLISHERS

It was the first day of kindergarten.

"Yoon, stand there so I can take
your picture."

Mom wanted Yoon to smile, but she
couldn't. She was too nervous.

"Boys come here, girls go over there."
As soon as her teacher asked, Yoon went to line up.

"No, boys are there," the girl with the purple jacket said to Yoon.
Then the girl in the plaid skirt looked over.
"Teacher, aren't boys supposed to be on that side?"

"Over here," called the boy with the turquoise vest.
And then the boy with the tie told Yoon, "Boys are on this side!"
Finally, the boy in the green shirt spoke up.
"No, she's a girl. She lives in our building."
But everyone else was talking, and no one heard him.

"I'm not a boy!"

Yoon shouted.
And then she started to cry.

"Smile!"
And she didn't stop crying for a long, long time.

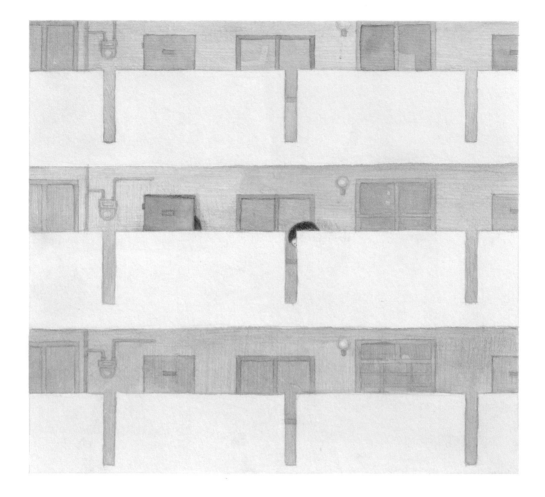

"Who called you a boy? You don't look like a boy! You're my beautiful girl!"
Mom tried to make Yoon feel better, but it didn't work.

"*Do* I look like a boy?"

She tried on some of Mom's things.
"How's this?"

Then some of Sister's favorites.
Finally …

..."It's perfect!"
Yoon put on the headband and looked in the mirror.
The pretend hair tickled her cheeks.
A little of her real hair showed, but it looked good.
No one could think she was a boy!

The next morning,
Sister was searching
for something.
"Mom, have you seen
my special headband?"

Yoon pretended not to hear, and rushed out to school.
"Bye!"
"Yoon, wait!"

She had a wonderful day at school.
No one called her a boy.
No one told her to go stand on the other side.

"Wheeee!"

Kindergarten was terrific.

But Sister had been looking for something.
"Oh, there's my headband!"

The next day, Yoon searched through her school bag.
"Where is it?"

"What if people think I'm a boy again?"

"Yoon, what are you doing? Come play jump rope!"

"Not last night, but the night before..."

Yoon forgot all about the special headband.

That night, she drew a picture in her journal,
and fell asleep thinking of her friends.
"There's Lee, Yoo-Jin, Jeong, Kyung-Yeon,
Choi, Seung-Kyu, Cho, Eun-Young, Kim,
Joon-Woo……"